Adapted by Jasmine Jones
Based on the series created by Terri Minsky
Part one is based on a teleplay written
by Doug Tuber and Tim Maile.
Part two is based on a teleplay written
by Doug Tuber and Tim Maile.

EGMONT

First published in the USA 2003
by Disney Press
First published in Great Britain 2003
by Egmont Books Limited,
239 Kensington High Street, London, W8 6SA

Published by arrangement with Disney Press,
114 Fifth Avenue, New York, New York 10011-5690

Copyright © 2003 Disney Enterprises, Inc.

ISBN 1 4052 0510 5

3 5 7 9 10 8 6 4 2

A CIP catalogue record for this title is available from the British Library

Printed and bound in the UK

PART ONE

CHAPTER ONE

"Mmmpph." Lizzie McGuire bit back a groan as she blinked up at one of her best friends, Miranda Sanchez. Lizzie was lying flat on her back in art class, and—naturally— all of the other students were gaping at her, openmouthed. Even Lizzie's snobby ex-friend, Kate Sanders, was glaring at her with narrowed eyes and a tense scowl. Not that Lizzie cared about what Kate thought. This was all her fault, anyway.

"Are you okay?" Miranda bent over Lizzie with a worried frown.

For a moment, Lizzie just gazed blankly at her best friend. What could she say? She was bruised, she was humiliated, and she was smeared with so much green paint that she looked like an escapee from the Saint Patrick's Day Parade. Not that it was Saint Patrick's Day. Or anywhere close.

"I cannot believe you did that," Lizzie's other best friend, Gordo, put in. It usually took a lot to impress Gordo, but right now his eyes were wide with respect.

"Are you sure you're okay?" Miranda repeated anxiously.

Okay?! This is so not okay. Believe it or not, when i got ready for school this morning, i wasn't aiming for leprechaun chic.

Lizzie let out a moan and swiped at the paint on her face. Oh, great. Now she'd managed to smear it. Perfect. That was the thing about this day—the minute Lizzie thought that it couldn't possibly get any worse or more humiliating . . . it did. She made no move to get up. Maybe I can just stay here, under the table, for the next few weeks or so, she thought. That way, she wouldn't have to face the rest of the school looking like the Glob from Planet Slime.

if you're wondering what happened to me, we have to go all the way back to this morning. But basically what happened is School Picture Day.

The day had started out perfectly normal.

When Lizzie's alarm clock went off, she slapped the snooze button groggily, as usual, then rolled over to enjoy another ten minutes of sleep. When the alarm went off again, she slapped it, again. Lizzie repeated this ritual three more times before finally giving up, climbing out of bed, and staggering to the shower. Perfectly normal.

Lizzie emerged from her shower, feeling much better. That is, she felt better . . . until she happened to check the calendar by her mirror. Oh, no. It can't be, she thought as she stared at the date. But it was. Yes—it was Picture Day. She had completely forgotten!

This was a fashion emergency of the highest order! After all, Lizzie thought, I can't just wear any old outfit on Picture Day. She needed something cool. Something fabulous. Something that screamed, "I'll look great in wallet size!" But as she stood in front of her closet in her blue terry-cloth bathrobe, one thing became perfectly clear.

"I have absolutely nothing to wear!" Lizzie wailed, flipping through outfit after outfit. "No," she said as she looked at a red checked blouse. "No," she said to a pair of blue-and-green-striped capris. "No, no, no, no!"

Just then, the phone rang. Lizzie dove for the cordless that was sitting on her night-stand, hoping desperately that it was Miranda. Miranda had good taste and she was brutally honest—and those were the two most important qualities to look for when you wanted to ask someone for fashion advice. "Hello?" Lizzie said eagerly.

"Hey." Lizzie's face fell. It was Gordo. Gordo was smart and he was funny—but he was definitely not the universe's greatest fashion consultant. His idea of a cool outfit was a bowling shirt with the name HAL over the pocket. "Could you check in your living room and see if I left my Hacky Sack over there?" Gordo asked.

Lizzie rolled her eyes. Did Gordo seriously think that she was going to trudge downstairs and search under the couch for his dumb Hacky Sack—*again?* No way. Especially not when she was having a clothing emergency! On the other hand, it was no use arguing with Gordo. He'd just hound her until she gave in. Lizzie decided to humor him. "Sure," she said into the phone. She waited a moment or two, then said, "It's not here, sorry." Her phone beeped. "Oh, hang on—I've got Call Waiting." Lizzie clicked over to the other line. "Hello?"

"It's me," Miranda said.

"Good!" Lizzie said into the receiver. "Talk me through a clothing crisis."

"What about your denim thing?" Miranda suggested.

Lizzie pictured herself in her black denim jeans and matching jean jacket. It had been her favorite outfit—for about two weeks. Then she got over it. "Too Shania Twain," she said.

Miranda laughed, just as the phone beeped again.

"Hold on—" Lizzie told her friend, "Call Waiting." She pushed the FLASH button. "Hello?"

"You hung up on me," Gordo complained. "You didn't look for the Hacky Sack, did you?"

Lizzie frowned at the receiver. Sometimes, having a supersmart friend who didn't care about clothes could be really annoying. "Gordo, I'm in the middle of a fashion meltdown," she explained.

"All righty, then," Gordo said, giving in. "Chicks . . ." he grumbled, clicking off.

Lizzie pressed the FLASH button again.

"That was Gordo," she told Miranda. "He's obsessing about his Hacky Sack."

Miranda gave a slight snort. "Boys," she griped.

Suddenly, Lizzie's door burst open, and her annoying little brother, Matt, poked his head into her room. He was already dressed for school. "Lizzie, I need the phone," he said.

Lizzie crinkled her nose and put her hand over the receiver. Matt was under the mistaken impression that she cared about what he wanted. "Well, that's a big problem for you," Lizzie told him, then turned her attention back to the phone. "You're so lucky you've got that Delia's outfit," Lizzie said to Miranda as she flopped onto her bed. Miranda had ordered a supercute orange tank top and zebra-striped skirt from the on-line catalog a couple of weeks ago.

"Three dollars an hour to clean Mrs.

Fernelius's backyard isn't exactly *luck*," Miranda said, shuddering.

Lizzie had to admit that this was true. Mrs. Fernelius was seriously tidiness-challenged. Her yard had been full of old appliances, weeds, and a horrible, slavering dog with halitosis. According to Miranda, the place would have given Martha Stewart a seizure.

Matt was still hovering. "Lizzie—phone!" he shouted.

Lizzie ignored him. "I was thinking more of a Sarah Michelle Gellar thing," she said into the receiver. "Powerful, but still cute." She imagined herself in a black shirt and a pair of leather pants, kicking some serious butt. "Or something classy, like Gwyneth at the Oscars." Lizzie smiled at the mental image of herself walking down the red carpet in a gorgeous pink silk evening gown. Hmm. Maybe that outfit was a little over the top for

Hillridge Junior High School. It would probably never survive the bus ride.

"Phone-phone-phone-phone!" Matt's annoying voice cut into Lizzie's daydream.

Lizzie grabbed a pillow from her bed and hurled it at her brother's head. He ducked behind her door, and the pillow bounced harmlessly away. Matt stuck his tongue out at Lizzie as she looked around her room for something else to throw. Did he have to be so immature—especially during an emergency?

"What about that red top you just got?" Miranda suggested.

"Oh, the halter?" Lizzie said eagerly. Suddenly, her full attention was back on the phone, instead of on her brother. "With a bare midriff and my black hip-huggers? That would be so 'Oops, I Did It Again!'" Lizzie could just picture herself decked out like Britney Spears . . . minus the headset.

"Mom! Dad!" Matt shouted. He ran out into the hall and leaned over the banister. "Lizzie's talking about dressing like Britney Spears! Man, she's *hot*," he added as he walked back to Lizzie's door.

Lizzie narrowed her eyes at her little brother. Oh, great. She could already hear her parents' feet pounding up the stairs. Ugh—she knew where this was going. Thanks to Matt, it would take Lizzie at least forty-five minutes of begging, pleading, promises, and coercion to convince her parents to let her wear the red halter to school . . . and that was only if she was *lucky*. "Code Blue," Lizzie said to Miranda. "I'll call you back." She clicked off the phone. "Three . . . two . . ." Lizzie began the familiar Parental Lecture countdown. "One—"

Right on time, Lizzie's mom and dad appeared in her doorway.

"Honey?" Mrs. McGuire asked as she stepped into Lizzie's room. She peered at her daughter over the top of her rectangular glasses. "Do we need to talk about this?"

"Britney Spears," Mr. McGuire said, frowning. "She's the one who got all developed, right?"

Matt lunged toward the phone and plucked it out of Lizzie's hand. "Thank you," he singsonged as he walked out the door. Lizzie glared after him.

"I don't want her going to school looking like that," Mr. McGuire said to his wife.

Lizzie rolled her eyes. Hel-lo? Had her parents even seen Britney Spears lately? She and Lizzie had different . . . um . . . body types.

i couldn't possibly look like Britney for at least five more years and, like, five million sit-ups.

Still, Lizzie knew that argument wasn't going to hold much water with her parents. It was better to get them off the topic entirely. "Matt's exaggerating," Lizzie said soothingly. "I was just talking to Miranda about what to wear for my school picture."

"I thought you were going to wear the sweater Gammy McGuire sent you for Christmas," Mrs. McGuire said. She yanked open Lizzie's dresser drawer and started rummaging through it.

"Hey, that's right," Lizzie's dad said—"the red one."

Lizzie bit her lip. "Oh. Um, I'd sort of changed my mind," she said quickly.

Mrs. McGuire finally found the sweater squashed into a ball at the back of the drawer. She held it up and smoothed it out, so that Lizzie could see it in all of its glory. Lizzie gulped. The bright red sweater had scratchy lace at the neck and sleeves, but what made it truly horrendous was that there was a gigantic satin unicorn appliquéd to the front. It wasn't that the sweater was ugly. It was *repulsive*. As in, the fashion police are coming for you, and they're going to put you away *for life*. But how could you explain something like that to your parents? Her dad's idea of the height of fashion was a pair of khakis and a shirt with no stains on it.

"You were so excited when you got it," Mrs. McGuire went on. "Why wouldn't you wear it?"

Maybe because it's hideous and makes me look like a cookie elf.

Lizzie stifled a groan, wishing that she hadn't been such a good actress on Christmas morning. Why couldn't she have just pitched a fit over the ugly sweater then and there, like her nemesis, Kate, would have done? But no—she'd gone on and on about how great the sweater was. She had even written Gammy McGuire an elaborate thank-you note in which she'd promised to wear the sweater on Picture Day.

Dumb Christmas spirit.

Lizzie couldn't tell her parents that she'd been lying all along. How was she going to get out of this? "Um," Lizzie hedged, "I just thought it was kind of warm to wear a sweater."

"Nah, it's cool out," Mr. McGuire said. He looked Lizzie in the eye. "It'd mean an awful lot to Gammy McGuire," he added.

"It's just . . ." Lizzie groped for a reason—any reason—not to wear the sweater.

"C'mon, Lizzie," Lizzie's mom urged.

"Gammy's not getting any younger. Who knows how much longer she'll be with us?"

Lizzie stared at her mom. "She's only sixty-one," Lizzie protested. "She teaches windsurfing!" Honestly, Lizzie couldn't believe that her parents were turning on the guilt machine. It was hardly like her grandmother was at death's door, or something. "And *her* mom is still alive."

But Mrs. McGuire just handed Lizzie the sweater without another word. Her dad folded his arms across his chest. Obviously, there was no getting out of this one. Lizzie was going to have to go to school as a major fashion Don't . . . and there was nothing she could do about it.

CHAPTER TWO

"What do you *mean* you didn't do the math homework?" Matt demanded into the phone as he walked down the stairs. "I'm supposed to get it from you." At the other end of the line, Matt's good friend, Oscar, babbled something about Family Movie Night. "I don't care if *Angels in the Outfield* was on last night!" Matt cried in exasperation. "I'm going to get in trouble without that homework. Thanks a lot, ya *muggle*."

Matt put his palm to his head. He'd already missed three homework assignments, and Ms. McGee had warned him that if he didn't hand in another one, she would have to call his parents.

But Oscar had even more bad news. "There's going to be a pop quiz, too?" Matt cried. "I'm toast!" He groaned. "There's no way I can go to school today." Just then, Matt heard his parents and his sister coming down the stairs. He said good-bye and hung up quickly.

"What if the pictures are in front of a red backdrop?" Lizzie protested as she walked into the kitchen. She was still trying to think of any excuse not to wear the sweater. "My head will just be floating there."

"I'm sure it will be a neutral background," Mrs. McGuire assured her daughter. "And it's an adorable sweater. Don't you think so, Matt?"

"Oooh, I think I'm going to throw up," Matt said, groaning loudly.

"Don't make fun of your sister's sweater, Matt," Mr. McGuire told him. "Gammy McGuire loves you kids."

"No—" Matt explained. "I don't feel good." He looked up at his mom with a wide-eyed, pitiful expression. "I think I'm sick," he wailed, doubling over.

Lizzie rolled her eyes, but Matt didn't even glance in her direction.

"Oh, boy, let me feel your forehead," Mrs. McGuire said. She put her palm against his forehead. "You *are* warm," she admitted, "but I can't tell if you have a fever. You'd better go back upstairs. I'll come up and take your temperature."

Matt moaned loudly and trudged upstairs, clutching his stomach. Lizzie's mom and dad looked at each other skeptically.

Lizzie sighed, and collapsed into a chair at the breakfast table. She knew that Matt was probably faking, but she didn't care. She had much bigger problems right now. Lizzie considered asking her mom for a paper sack. That way, she could cut out two eye holes and wear it over her head, and no one would know who the girl in the unicorn sweater was. It wasn't a perfect solution, but it had potential. . . .

"You'd better get some breakfast in you," Mrs. McGuire said to Lizzie. "And don't worry—you look really cute in that sweater. It's going to be a big hit." She smiled reassuringly at her daughter.

Lizzie looked down at the sweater, hopefully. Maybe it wasn't really as bad as she thought. Maybe nobody would even notice it.

Yeah, right.

Lizzie knew the minute that she walked up to

the bus stop that she had made a mistake. A huge, horrible, potentially life-altering mistake. It was written all over Miranda's face.

"What?" Lizzie asked, hoping that her friend would tell her that she really didn't look as bad as she knew she did.

"Nothing," Miranda said quickly. "It's just—that's not really 'Oops, I Did It Again.'" She pointed at Lizzie's satin unicorn. "That's just '*Oops.*'"

Lizzie sighed. At least she could always count on Miranda to be honest. "My stupid brother got my parents involved," she confessed. "They picked it out."

Miranda winced sympathetically. "Ouch."

The school bus pulled up and the doors opened with a hiss. "My grandmother gave me this sweater for Christmas," Lizzie explained as they boarded the bus. Kids giggled and snickered as Lizzie walked past. Half of them craned their heads to look at her as she slid into her seat. "Will you stop staring at me?" Lizzie demanded. A few turned back around, but most of them just kept gaping. Not that Lizzie blamed them. The sweater was kind of like a train wreck . . . it was so horrifying that you just couldn't look away from it. "It's fine—it's just a picture," Lizzie said quickly. She wasn't sure who she was trying to convince, Miranda or herself.

"It is *not* just a picture," Miranda protested. "We're in junior high now. These pictures don't just go home in an envelope—they get published in the *yearbook*."

Just then, a pudgy kid drinking from a small carton of milk walked down the aisle past them. The minute he saw Lizzie, he choked. Milk exploded all over his face—and about half of it poured out from his nostrils. The kid behind him slapped him on the back as he continued to choke. Lizzie wanted to crawl under her seat and hide.

"Your sweater gave Rudy Velasco nose milk," Miranda said to Lizzie. "This is serious. This picture will be seen by everybody, forever."

"Forever?" Lizzie repeated, feeling kind of queasy.

"Forever. I mean, haven't you seen your parents' yearbook pictures?" Miranda's dark eyes were round with horror.

Lizzie bit her lip. Miranda had a point. Lizzie had seen her parents' yearbook pictures, and they put the *ug* in *ugly*. Lizzie's mom had worn dental headgear, and Lizzie's dad looked as though his nose were trying to conquer the kingdom of his face. When Lizzie had first seen the pictures, she'd laughed so hard that she had actually given herself a stomachache. Did she really want her picture to have the same effect on her own children someday? "I've got to get home and change," Lizzie said quickly.

"Go!" Miranda urged.

Lizzie stood up and bolted to the front of the bus. Just as she reached the last step, the bus doors hissed shut in her face. She was trapped! Lizzie pounded against the glass, but it was no use. The bus had pulled away from the curb. Lizzie was on her way to school—for better or for worse.

Matt gazed up at his mom with big, gloomy eyes as he laid on the couch in the living room. He had a digital thermometer in his mouth, and a pillow propped behind his head.

"Yeah," Mrs. McGuire said into the cordless phone as she paced around the living room. "I'm taking his temperature right now." She held the receiver against her chest. "Your father's very concerned about you," she told Matt in a low voice as she plucked the thermometer from his mouth. "Oh, wow." Matt's mom shook her head and frowned disapprovingly as she read his temperature. "A hundred and two. You stay put, young man— you are not going to school today." Mrs. McGuire walked out of the living room and into the kitchen. "Yup, a hundred and two on the nose," she whispered into the phone. "You're probably right about the flashlight trick." She peeked back into the living room, hiding behind the door frame. Matt was grinning as he pulled a flashlight from behind a sofa cushion and held the thermometer against it.

"And there it is," Mrs. McGuire said into the phone triumphantly. "He's *definitely* faking. Where do they learn these things? Is there some Kid Handbook we don't know about?"

"So what are you going to do?" Mr. McGuire asked.

"Oh, don't worry," Mrs. McGuire told him. "I'll definitely 'take care' of him. See you tonight." She clicked off the phone and walked into the living room. She pretended not to notice as Matt quickly turned off the flashlight and shoved it between the sofa cushions. "How are you feeling, sweetie?" she asked.

Matt just moaned.

"Aw," Mrs. McGuire said sympathetically. "You know what you need?" she asked as she straightened the blanket tucked around Matt's legs. "Some soup."

"Chicken noodle?" Matt asked, gazing up at her hopefully.

Mrs. McGuire smiled at him and shook her head. "Borscht," she said, tweaking Matt playfully on the nose. "That's cold beet soup. You need the vitamin C."

Matt grimaced as his mom kissed him on the forehead and walked into the kitchen to make soup. "I hate beets," he grumbled.

CHAPTER THREE

"Yo—Gordon," Ethan Craft said as he leaned casually against the locker next to Gordo's. Ethan gave his glossy dark blond hair a flip, and looked down at Gordon with an intimidating glare.

"Oh, hey," Gordo said cautiously as he pulled his heavy social studies textbook from the top shelf of his locker. "What's up?"

"You have your picture taken yet?" Ethan asked.

Gordo frowned. "No," he said slowly. "Fourth period. Why?"

"We've got this really cool plan," Ethan

explained. "When the guys get their pictures taken, at the last minute we're going to do this—" He pointed to his face.

Gordo's eyebrows drew together in confusion. He closed his locker and looked at Ethan more carefully. "Going to do what?" Gordo asked.

"This." Ethan pointed to his face again. He was stone-faced. "Isn't that great?" Ethan asked, dropping the serious look, and giving Gordo a huge grin.

"Oh, yeah," Gordo lied as he fell into step beside Ethan. "Awesome."

"We're going to be a bunch of straight-up playas," Ethan went on as he strutted slowly down the hall. Other kids scurried out of his way. "*That'll* show the faculty."

"Show them what?" Gordo asked.

Ethan shrugged. "Um . . . that we mean business. So, you in?"

Gordo hesitated, and Ethan poked him in

the shoulder. "You better not be against us on this, dude. You gotta survive at this school, and it's a long time till summer."

Gordo dug his fists into his pockets. "I might not even get my picture taken," he said to Ethan. "I'm going to tell my teacher I grew up with Kalahari Desert bushmen, so I believe that if someone takes my picture, it'll steal my soul from me and I'll be doomed to eternal wandering."

Ethan thought about that for a minute. "You're weird," he said.

Gordo smiled as he watched Ethan shuffle away, then headed over to Lizzie's locker, where Lizzie and Miranda were huddled together, whispering.

"You don't get your picture taken till sixth period," Miranda was saying. "There's gotta be somebody you can borrow an outfit from by then."

"Hey, what's going on?" Gordo asked as he walked up to them. Lizzie turned to face him, and Gordo winced at what he saw. "Whoa."

Lizzie sighed. "Long story, Gordo," she said.

"I got time," Gordo told her.

Taking a deep breath, Lizzie ran through everything that had happened to her that morning, from her interaction with Matt to Rudy Velasco's nose milk. "And when I got to school, no one would swap sweaters with me," Lizzie finished.

Gordo pressed his lips together for a moment, clearly considering the story. "I didn't know your grandmother taught wind-surfing," he said finally.

"Thanks, Gordo, that's really helpful," Lizzie told him, then turned back to Miranda. "You know, every school picture I've ever taken has been colossally lame. Sixth grade— braces. Fifth grade—bee sting on my nose.

Fourth grade—missing tooth." She shook her head at the memory of the string of hopelessly pathetic photos that her parents had in their wallets. "For once, I am going to look good in my school picture," Lizzie declared.

"Why is everyone so obsessed with these pictures?" Gordo wanted to know. "You're freaking because of a sweater."

She couldn't believe that Gordo was criticizing her—wasn't he the one who had been obsessing about his Hacky Sack that very morning? "How I look in this picture has a lot to do with how everybody in school thinks about me," Lizzie snapped.

"You really care about what a bunch of jocks and cheerleaders think about you?" Gordo asked.

Lizzie and Miranda looked at each other. "Yeah," they chorused.

Gordo looked at the ceiling and sighed.

"How you look in a picture doesn't mean you're a good person. I'm studying John Wilkes Booth in my history class—he looked good in pictures, and he was kind of a jerk."

it can be a little tough when one of your two best friends says things that are kind of bizarre.

Lizzie and Miranda exchanged meaningful glances.

"Well, John Wilkes Booth wasn't trying to get Danny Kessler to like him," Miranda shot back.

When both of your best friends do, you just learn to deal with it.

There had been enough photo talk. Now it was time to do something about it. "I gotta go find an outfit," Lizzie said, steering Miranda down the hall. Gordo gave them a small wave, and headed off to class in the opposite direction.

As Lizzie and Miranda turned the corner, Miranda stopped in her tracks. Halfway up the hall, Kate was standing at her locker. She was wearing an orange tank top and a zebra-print skirt—exactly the same outfit Miranda had on. Uh-oh. Lizzie knew that Kate wasn't the kind of person who would get a laugh out of something like that. And neither was Miranda.

Kate's best friend, Claire Miller, saw Miranda first, and her mouth dropped open in shock. Kate turned to see what Claire was looking at. When Kate saw Miranda, her green eyes narrowed, and she slammed her locker door with an earsplitting bang.

Throughout the animal kingdom, it's a well-known fact that males fiercely compete to establish themselves within the herd.

Miranda squared her shoulders and slowly walked toward Kate. Lizzie bit her lip as a shiver of fear ran down her spine. This was not good.

But in junior high, girls get in on the action, too.

"You're *not* wearing that," Kate said as she squared off against Miranda.

Miranda pretended to be shocked. "I'm not?" she asked sarcastically. Then she leaned toward Kate, warningly. "It feels like I *am*."

"I looked for this outfit for weeks," Kate went on. "You'd better change before sixth period."

"Okay," Miranda said slowly. "I'll change. I'll pretend you're not a big . . ."—she held out her hands, clearly searching for the perfect insult—"snot-faced . . . snot-head," she improvised.

Just then, the bell rang. Kate brushed by Miranda, knocking against her shoulder— hard. "You are not wearing that," she growled, and strutted off. Claire followed her.

Lizzie cocked an eyebrow at her friend. "Snot-faced snot-head?" she asked.

"Okay," Miranda said, knowing her comeback had not been first-class. "But I think I made my point."

Maybe so, Lizzie thought as she followed her friend to class. And she had to admit that she admired her best friend's courage. Miranda had really stood up for herself—and she had been right. But somehow, Lizzie didn't think that was going to make much difference to Kate.

CHAPTER FOUR

"Okay, I'm done," Matt said as he pushed away his empty, purple-stained soup bowl. It had taken him almost forty-five minutes to choke down the beet soup.

"That's my little trouper," Mrs. McGuire said in a chipper voice. "I bet you feel better now."

"Yeah," Matt said quickly, then thought for a moment. "I mean, *no*," he corrected himself, with a low moan. "I still feel pretty sick."

Trotting into the living room, Matt plopped down on the couch and picked up the remote control. Cartoons sprang to life on the screen as Matt grinned and leaned back against the plump couch pillows.

"No, no, no," Mrs. McGuire said as she followed him into the room. She picked up another remote and clicked off the cartoons. "What you need is some peace and quiet."

Matt frowned and clicked the TV back on. Mrs. McGuire turned it off. Matt turned it on again. Finally, Matt's mom grabbed the remote from his hand and placed both remotes on the table, out of reach. Then she leaned over and felt Matt's forehead. "Oh, my gosh, you're burning up!"

Matt frowned in confusion. "I am?" he said.

Mrs. McGuire nodded. "We've got to sweat this fever out of you."

Matt grimaced. "We do?" he asked dubiously.

"You get upstairs," Matt's mom said. "I'm going to set up the vaporizer, bundle you up in the old wool blanket—"

"But that *itches*," Matt complained.

"Only if you move around," Mrs. McGuire reassured him. "And you'll be wrapped up so tight, you won't be able to."

Matt cast a longing glance at the television set. "So, after I sweat, I can watch TV?" he asked. His mom nodded, and Matt smiled to himself. "Can I get a drink of water before we go upstairs?" he asked craftily, sneaking a quick look toward the kitchen.

Mrs. McGuire shrugged. "Sure," she said, "go ahead."

Matt hopped off the couch and shuffled into the kitchen. He pulled open the fridge and smiled when he saw the big can of jalapeño peppers on the middle shelf. "These always make Dad's head sweat," Matt said as he plucked a gigantic pepper from the can and popped it into his mouth. A moment later, his mouth dropped open. "Aaagh!" Matt shouted, reaching for the nearest bottle in the fridge. He unscrewed the top and took a big swig. "Ugh!" Matt gagged, and turned the bottle so that he could read the label. Prune juice!

Matt shook his head as he put the prune juice back into the fridge and sighed. He felt his forehead, which was covered in beads of sweat. "At least my plan worked—kind of," he said with a groan as he hobbled back into the living room.

"Aaargh!"

A brilliant burst of light came from the cafeteria, and a moment later, a kid staggered out, clearly blinded from the camera flash.

His eyes were crossed—he was half blind from the intense light. Gordo suppressed a shudder and shuffled forward. It was fourth period, and he was in the line to have his photograph taken.

"Hey, Gordo," Lizzie said as she walked up to him. She smiled at him weakly.

"No luck finding an outfit, huh?" Gordo asked, trying to avoid making eye contact with the offending unicorn.

"Plenty of luck," Lizzie said, rolling her eyes. "All *bad*. Oh—Bethany Adelstein says I can borrow her sunglasses so maybe people won't know who the poor little she-geek is." Lizzie folded her arms over the mythical creature in satin. Maybe I can just keep my arms like this for the rest of the day, she thought. Hmm . . . it was a possibility, although it would make it difficult to take a pop quiz, or use the bathroom.

"You gotta trust me," Gordo told her. "This picture is not important."

"It's not important to *you*," Lizzie replied. "It's important to *me*."

Gordo shrugged. "I just don't see why we should give in to peer pressure."

"Because we have peers!" Lizzie cried in exasperation. "And they put pressure on us! If it was just you and me, I wouldn't care how I look, but I have to live in this world."

"You look *fine*," Gordo told her.

Coming from the cafeteria, they heard a girl's voice wail. "But I wasn't ready yet!" A moment later, the door opened and a tall blond girl in headgear staggered out. She was wearing an embroidered top and two fluffy purple ponytail holders. It was *not* a good look.

Lizzie stared at her a moment, remembering her mom's hideous yearbook photo. "Nice try, Gordo," she said finally. "But I'm not going to let that happen to me." She gave him a wry little smile, then turned and walked away. She was on a mission. She had to find a new outfit.

She just had to.

The school photographer was a very large woman with a very bad attitude. She said, "Smile," the same way that a drill sergeant would say, "Drop and give me twenty." When she said, "Smile"—people smiled.

"Arrggh!" A kid screamed as the camera flashed with the brilliance of a solar flare.

"Next!" the photographer called as the kid rubbed his eyes and lurched away.

Gordo was next on line.

"Remember, Gordon—" Ethan said, leaning in toward Gordo menacingly. Ethan gave Gordo the stone-faced look. Then he glared at Gordo as he walked toward the photographer's stool.

"Okay, smile," the photographer commanded as Gordo settled in front of the neutral blue background.

Gordo hesitated, then gave the photographer a stern look.

The photographer frowned at him. "That is not a smile," she growled, her eyes bulging in disapproval. "Smile!"

Gordo glanced over at Ethan, who pointed to the grim expression on his face again. Gordo looked back at the photographer. She scowled at him. Gordo forced himself to smile.

"One . . ." The photographer said.

Gordo sat there, smiling stiffly, as he remembered what Ethan had said to him that morning: "You gotta survive at this school, and it's a long time till summer." Then an image of Lizzie flashed in his mind, and

Gordo could hear her, too. "How this picture comes out has a lot to do with how everybody in school thinks about me," she'd said.

"Two . . ." The photographer warned.

Gordo glanced over at Ethan. He was still stone-faced, and his eyes were narrowed warningly at Gordo. Gordo sighed.

"Three," the photographer said. Gordo dropped his smile the minute the camera flashed. The photographer grimaced as Ethan gave Gordo a thumbs-up. "Ugh," the photographer said, clearly disappointed with Gordo's expression. "Next."

Gordo shook his head as he stumbled away from the neutral background, his eyes throbbing from the brilliant flash.

Lizzie walked out onto the lunch patio, gnawing on her bottom lip. A cluster of girls glanced in her direction, then put their heads together, giggling. Lizzie could feel herself blushing. This sweater was completely ruining her life! She just *had* to find a way to ditch it. She'd take anything—anything! Even Larry Tudgeman's putty-colored shirt with the lime-green collar was starting to look good. Though Larry didn't have much fashion sense, something told Lizzie that she wouldn't be able to convince him to swap with her.

She just *had* to find someone who would.

Outfit, outift, who's got the outfit? Lisa Chung? She blew me off. . . . Allison Gendel? She smells like feet. . . . Tamara Scarpati . . . ?

Lizzie eyed Tamara for a minute. Sure, her outfit was cute. There was only one problem—

Tamara was about six feet tall. Lizzie had even heard a rumor that the New York Liberty women's basketball team was scouting her. Lizzie, on the other hand, was barely tall enough to reach the top shelf of her locker.

Yeah, like that's going to work.

Lizzie cast her eyes around the patio. There just had to be someone. . . .

Suddenly, her gaze landed on Parker McKenzie. Okay, so Parker's long-sleeved brown shirt wasn't exactly the height of fashion. But it was definitely better than what Lizzie had on. Of course, at this point, Lizzie would have settled for a burlap sack. Anything! Anything but this hideous sweater and its satin unicorn with the fake jewel eye!

Lizzie took a halting step toward Parker. This wasn't going to be easy. *She's hated me since I sat on her* Titanic *lunch box in the fifth grade,* Lizzie remembered, stopping in her tracks. *I'd rather die than go crawling to her.*

But Lizzie was out of options. And if she didn't ask Parker for her shirt, Lizzie just *might* die—of embarrassment. Was it really worth the risk? Forcing down a shudder, Lizzie walked over to where Parker was sitting, picking at the food on her lunch tray.

"Hey, Parker," Lizzie said brightly. She peered down at Parker's clunky brown oxfords. "Great shoes!"

Parker rolled her eyes and tossed her long brown hair over her shoulder. "Uh-huh."

Okay, this wasn't starting well. Lizzie decided to lay it on a little thicker. "I mean it," she said, in the sincerest voice she could possibly fake. "Those are just, like, *majorly* fabulous."

Parker stared at her tray, as though lasagna was the most fascinating lunch in the universe. "Whatever," she said. "Yours are okay, too, I guess."

"You wanna borrow 'em?" Lizzie asked eagerly. "'Cause you can, anytime. And maybe I could borrow something from you. Like maybe your . . . blouse."

"Oh, that's right," Parker said, her voice bored. "I heard you were *begging* people for their clothes. Everyone thinks that's really creepy." Parker stood up and walked away. She didn't even take her lunch with her.

Lizzie gritted her teeth. Stupid Parker McKenzie. Lizzie wished that Parker had brought her lunch in her *Titanic* lunch box, so that she could sit on it all over again.

Your shoes bite!

* * *

Matt walked out of the bathroom, clutching his stomach. He'd brushed his teeth five times, and had even gargled with mouthwash, but he could still taste the prune juice–jalapeño blend he'd swallowed.

"Tummy still jumbled?" Matt's mom asked sympathetically.

"Um . . . no?" Matt guessed.

"Good," Mrs. McGuire said. "You can help me wind some yarn." She pulled an enormous basket of brightly colored yarn from behind the couch and began sorting through it.

Matt's shoulders slumped. "Do I have to?" he whined as he trudged to the couch and sat down next to his mother.

"Only till your body cools down," his mom said. "You still seem a little feverish." Mrs. McGuire positioned Matt's wrists upright, and started winding some yarn around them.

She wound the yarn around and around . . . around and around . . . around and around. . . .

Matt glanced at the clock on the wall. The seconds ticked by slowly. After a while, Matt's arms began to look like a sweater on two sticks. And still Mrs. McGuire kept on winding the yarn.

"Um, could I get some soda crackers?" Matt asked in his most pathetic-sounding voice. "For my stomach?"

"Sure, honey," Mrs. McGuire said. She tucked the ball of yarn into Matt's hands. He hauled himself off the couch as well as he could, given that his arms were practically knitted together.

"As soon as you cool down, you can watch some TV," she promised.

Matt scurried into the kitchen and pulled the yarn off his arms. Then he pressed the button on the ice-maker and cupped his hands underneath as a few ice cubes fell into them. Matt rubbed the ice against his face. Then he tucked the ice cubes into his pajama bottoms.

Matt stifled a scream. "Maybe . . . that's . . . a little . . . *too* . . . cold," he muttered.

CHAPTER FIVE

Thud! A metallic clang rang through the hallway as Lizzie banged the back of her head against her locker door. *Thud! Thud!* She was completely out of options. She was going to have to wear this sweater—and the photograph of it would haunt her for the rest of eternity. There's no way out, Lizzie thought, as she banged her head against the locker. No way out. No way out!

"Come on," Gordo said. He tugged on her

elbow, snapping Lizzie out of her waking nightmare.

"What?" Lizzie demanded.

"Come on," Gordo repeated, "I want to show you something."

"Gordo, I'm busy," Lizzie snapped. "And this is important." She stared into space for a minute, then started banging her head against the locker again.

"My thing's more important," Gordo assured her. He gave her a gentle little shove, and Lizzie finally gave in and followed him down the hall. After all, it wasn't like she had anything better to do. She could always go back to her head-banging later.

Gordo stopped in front of his locker. What's this? Lizzie wondered as Gordo pulled open the metal door. She stepped closer . . . and then she saw it. Lizzie gasped. Clothes. Gordo's locker was crammed with clothes!

And not just any clothes—these were retrochic, totally hip clothes. The locker seemed to radiate with a brilliant glow as a choir of angels sang from on high. It was as though Lizzie had been shown the gateway to Fashion Nirvana. Her jaw dropped. Had she just died and gone to clothing heaven?

"Take your pick," Gordo told her.

"Where did you get these?" Lizzie asked breathlessly.

Gordo shrugged. "The drama department is putting on a play," he explained. "The girl in charge of costumes owed me a favor. She needed a partner for her clog-dance class."

Lizzie imagined Gordo skipping around in a pair of high-water pants and clogs, and grinned. That was a pretty big favor for him to call in. And he'd done it just to help her with her clothing crisis? "I thought you thought this whole school picture thing was stupid," she said.

"I do," Gordo admitted. "But certain events happened that made me realize that stupid things can still be important."

Lizzie's grin widened. "You caved on the Ethan Craft–stone-faced thing, didn't you?"

"Yeah," Gordo said, his shoulders slumping a little. "But I still think who you are as a person is more important than how you look in a picture."

Lizzie brightened. "So, as long as I'm a good person, it's okay to want to look pretty?" she asked him.

Gordo thought about that for a moment. "Yeah, it's okay," he decided.

"Thanks." Lizzie reached into the locker and pulled out a sleeveless shirt. "I want the white one." She held it up. "This is so cool. So retro . . . So"—she looked at Gordo and smiled—"absolutely perfect."

Gordo smiled back, and Lizzie had to resist the urge to hug him. Who would have thought that a guy like Gordo would be her fashion savior?

Maybe there was something to those bowling shirts, after all.

Matt sat hunched on the couch, wrapped in a warm blanket, with the digital thermometer in his mouth. He didn't even bother to hold it against the flashlight.

He barely had the energy to look up as his mom breezed into the living room. "As long as you're sitting, we can do fraction drills," she said brightly as she slid the thermometer out of his mouth. But when she glanced at it, her eyebrows flew up. "A hundred and three!" she cried.

Matt nodded feebly.

Mrs. McGuire leaned over and felt his

forehead, which was damp with perspiration. "You really *are* hot," she said, her eyebrows drawn together in a worried frown. "Oh, honey, how'd you get so sick?" she asked, wrapping her arms around Matt.

"Don't know . . ." Matt croaked. "Hot peppers . . . Ice in my pants . . ." He shook his head, as though he were remembering a bad dream. "No more yarn!" he cried.

"Oh, my gosh, you're delirious!" his mom said. "Lie down, lie down!" she urged, tucking a pillow behind Matt's head. "I'm going to go make you the soup you like. Then I'm running to the store for some ginger ale." She wrapped the blanket more tightly around Matt as he lay back on the couch. She looked at him for a minute. "You don't feel good, do you?" she asked gently.

"I feel awful," Matt admitted weakly.

Mrs. McGuire gave him a kiss on the

forehead and hurried into the kitchen to make soup. Matt watched her leave, then closed his eyes wearily. "Being sick is complicated," he murmured, just before he fell asleep.

Lizzie added a peach to her charcoal drawing of a bowl of fruit and sighed. Whenever she drew a still life, it came out looking like a bowl of lumpy oatmeal. Why did she even bother? She peeked over at Miranda's easel, which was propped up next to her own. At least Miranda wasn't having much luck, either. The pineapple she was drawing looked seriously weird. Like it had racing stripes, or something.

Miranda looked over and smiled approvingly at Lizzie's outfit. "Perfect outfit," she said. "Very Kirsten Dunst meets South Beach. We are going to look so good in our pictures!"

"Thanks to Gordo, I'm actually looking forward to next period," Lizzie admitted.

Gordo raised an eyebrow. "Your pineapple looks like a skunk," he told Miranda.

Lizzie looked at Miranda's pineapple again. "Hey, it does!" she said, giggling.

Miranda groaned. "How come we have to draw fruit, anyway?" she complained. "I want to draw 'N Sync!"

"You make a pineapple look like a skunk," Gordo countered—"imagine what you'd do to Justin Timberlake."

Lizzie laughed and looked up to see whether everyone else was having as much trouble as she and her friends were. Across the room, she saw Kate whispering to a short, pudgy guy named Ed. They were both out of their seats, standing by the paint closet. That was weird, Lizzie thought. Usually, Kate wouldn't have wanted to be caught dead talking to a nerdy guy like Ed.

"Why is Kate being all nice to Ed?" Lizzie

murmured, half to herself. Then she noticed the gigantic tub of green paint that Ed was holding. "And what's he doing with paint?" Everyone else in the class was drawing with charcoal. Come to think of it . . . why was Ed walking toward her and her friends with that crazy look in his eyes?

i know! Kate's got a plan! She's hired Ed to whack Miranda's outfit!

A chill ran down Lizzie's spine as Ed pulled the lid off the tub of paint.

Miranda worked hard for three months to get that outfit. Her class picture will be ruined!

Lizzie couldn't let this happen! But she felt as though she were frozen to her seat. She couldn't move—she couldn't even speak—as Ed got nearer.

"Hey, what are you doing?" Gordo asked, as Ed pulled back the paint and prepared to hurl it at Miranda.

Just then, Miranda looked up. When she saw what was happening, she screamed. The sound jolted Lizzie into action. She couldn't let Miranda's outfit go down!

"Miranda, look out!" Gordo shouted. But it was too late. Ed had flung the paint into the air!

"No-o-o-o-o!" Lizzie cried, diving in front of the vibrant green glob that was headed straight toward Miranda's orange tank top. The paint splattered all over Lizzie, and she crumpled to the floor in a messy, slime-colored heap. She lay there for a moment, flat on her back, staring up at her friends. She glanced around the room. Everyone was gaping at her. Kate gave her a special glare, but Lizzie ignored her. She even smiled a little. After all, Miranda's outfit was completely clean—there wasn't a speck of green paint anywhere on it. Kate's plan had failed.

"Are you okay?" Miranda asked, staring down at her friend.

"I cannot believe you did that," Gordo said.

i can't believe it, either. But Miranda would jump on a paint grenade for me. Besides, green's very in this season.

A week later, Lizzie and her friends were sitting at their usual lunch table, passing around the proofs for their photos. Lizzie actually laughed when she saw hers. She was covered in green paint—it was even in her hair. She was grinning and holding up the unicorn sweater. After all, she thought, why not? Lizzie had decided that she couldn't possibly look any worse than she already did. Besides, it wasn't like she was the only one whose picture came out weird. Kate had sneezed in the middle of her photo. And once Ethan had to face the drill-sergeant photographer, he'd given in and smiled goofily for the camera.

On the other hand, Miranda and Gordo both had taken perfect photos.

Miranda looked way awesome, and Gordo had turned out great. All moody and troubled, like Freddy Prinze Jr.

"You guys look amazing," Lizzie told them when she saw their proofs. "I can hardly wait to see the yearbook."

"Tell me about it," Miranda agreed. "You

may get elected Most Likely to Become a Swamp Creature."

Lizzie laughed. So she *did* look pretty bad in the picture—but she didn't care. Miranda looked great, and that was what mattered. Lizzie would take the paint dive again—any time. It had been totally worth it.

Like Gordo says, I'd rather be a good person than look good in a picture. Besides, I liked the way I looked—even if my parents won't be that enthusiastic.

I guess that's what Mom and Dad get for picking the outfit, Lizzie thought, as she studied her photo. Maybe next time, Britney Spears won't strike them as such a bad option.

Lizzie laughed out loud at the thought. Hey—a girl could dream, couldn't she?

Lizzie McGUiRE

PART TWO

CHAPTER ONE

Bang! Bang!

Lizzie and Miranda slammed open their lockers, not even bothering to say hello to Gordo, who was gathering his books and notebooks a few locker doors down. Lizzie stuffed her spiral English notebook into her locker roughly, as though she were angry at it—which she was.

"Hey, guys," Gordo said cheerfully.

Miranda let out an incomprehensible grunt, and slammed her locker door.

"Ooh, a grunt *and* a locker slam," Gordo said. "That can only mean one thing—somebody's got a book report due." He cocked an eyebrow knowingly.

Lizzie shuddered, then pulled her social studies textbook from her locker and closed the door with a dull, metallic clang.

"We have to write five pages on *The Red Pony*," Miranda griped.

"Yeah," Lizzie joined in. "There's a red pony. It belongs to a little boy. It dies. The end." She ticked the plot points off on her fingers and rolled her eyes. *Ugh.* Why did all of the books they read in school have to be so dull? Couldn't the teachers assign anything that had a good romance, or a thrilling mystery in it, or something? "*How* are we supposed to write five pages about that?" she demanded, folding her arms across her chest.

Gordo shrugged. "Double-space, and use

wide margins?" he suggested. Lizzie and Miranda shot him a disgusted look. "Well, you've got P.E. next," he went on, apologetically. "You don't have homework in that."

Lizzie groaned as she and her friends shuffled down the hall toward the gym. Honestly, sometimes Gordo could be such a boy. Didn't he understand that gym was the worst class ever? "Yeah," she told him sarcastically. "We just have to take a shower in front of two hundred girls who do nothing but judge."

"Yeah, and that's just plain fun," Miranda chimed in. She stopped in her tracks. "You know, I *really* don't feel like going. Maybe I'll tell Coach Kelly I'm sick, and get out of it."

Lizzie's eyebrows lifted in surprise. "Whoa—" she said, "look who's the rebel girl all of a sudden." The truth was, Lizzie hated it when Miranda ditched P.E. Everyone else in their class took their sports a little too seriously. When Miranda sat out, Lizzie had no one to complain to about the lameness of group athletics.

"Don't ditch P.E.," Gordo urged. "You *love* volleyball. You can smash every serve, and really take out your frustrations."

Yeah, volleyball, that's it.

"Oh, all right," Miranda said with a sigh. "But I'm warning you . . . don't stand under my spike."

"Don't worry," Lizzie told her. "I want you to take out your frustrations on the ball, not on *me*."

"Where's Coach Kelly?" Lizzie asked as she sat

down cross-legged between Gordo and Miranda. Most of the class was already there, sitting on the blue stretching mats that were laid out across the floor or on the bleachers, but their teacher was nowhere in sight.

"The word around the campfire is that she's participating in a national Iron Woman contest," Gordo said.

"That's just a dumb rumor that Danny Kessler made up," Miranda said with a snort. "I don't believe it for a minute."

Lizzie pressed her lips together, unsure. After all, Coach Kelly was a big woman. In Lizzie's opinion, she probably had a pretty good shot at a contest like that. But whether it was true or not, Coach Kelly's absence was probably good news. "Maybe they'll give us a free period," Lizzie suggested hopefully.

Miranda gave her friend a wry smile. "Keep dreaming," she said.

Just then, Mr. Dig walked into the gym, wearing an orange satin shirt, tight black pants, jazz shoes, and a headband. Mr. Dig was a regular substitute teacher at Hillridge Junior High School. He was fit and pretty good-looking, so the outfit didn't look as bizarre on him as it would have on most of Lizzie's other teachers. Still . . . it didn't bode well. Plus, he was carrying a boom box. Lizzie was almost sure that she could smell a freaky project coming on. Freaky projects were kind of Mr. Dig's "thing."

Mr. Dig walked to the front of the class and put down the boom box, then clapped his hands together enthusiastically. "Hey, guys, I'm filling in for Coach Kelly for a few weeks," he announced. "Instead of volleyball, we are going learn the gentle art of . . ." Mr. Dig struck a pose, and Lizzie tried to guess what he was going to say. Karate? Tai chi? Either one would be okay.

Please say something cool, Lizzie thought. Please say something easy. Please say—

"Dance," Mr. Dig said.

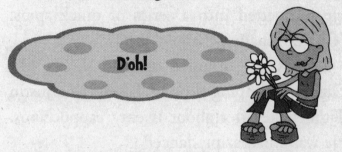

D'oh!

Lizzie sighed. This day was not looking up.

"You might find it a little weird to study dance in P.E.," Mr. Dig went on, "but dance is a very healthful physical activity."

Gordo leaned closer to Lizzie. "Mr. Dig teaches history. He teaches English," he muttered. "He has no business teaching us to dance."

Mr. Dig pressed a button on the boom box, and jazz music poured from the speakers. "Okay, everybody, watch this," Mr. Dig said, launching into a series of complicated dance steps. He leaped in the air, then moved into a jazz sequence, spreading his fingers wide and making them quiver. "Jazz, jazz, jazz. Hands!" He pirouetted into a series of quick spins. "Chaîné, chaîné, chaîné—leap!"

Lizzie's jaw dropped open in shock. Mr. Dig was jumping around faster than Justin Timberlake after about twenty cappuccinos. He was an amazing dancer!

Miranda lifted her eyebrows at Gordo. "You know, for a smart guy, you're wrong, like, ninety percent of the time."

"I was right about Vice Principal Kaplan's toupee," Gordo said defensively.

Lizzie rolled her eyes. Okay, so Gordo had been right about the toupee. Was she really supposed to be impressed? Mr. Kaplan looked like he was wearing a sweater on his head!

"Duh!" Miranda teased Gordo. She and Lizzie cracked up.

"Okay, Mr. Gordon . . ." Mr. Dig said, breaking into the friends' conversation.

Gordo looked up, guiltily. "Wha . . . me?" he asked. He looked behind him, as though he thought there might be another Mr. Gordon in the room.

Mr. Dig nodded. "Do exactly what I did," he said, gesturing for Gordo to come to the front of the class. "You will be graded. Go!"

Gordo jumped to his feet. "Umm . . ." he said, clearly wracking his brain for a way to get out of dancing in front of the entire class. Lizzie was certain that Gordo had no idea what Mr. Dig had just done—the man's feet had been a blur!

Mr. Dig laughed. "I'm just messing with you," he said.

Gordo heaved a relieved sigh and sat back down.

Lizzie had to press her lips together to keep

from giggling. Mr. Dig could be kind of strange—but he had a pretty good sense of humor. She had to admit that he'd really gotten Gordo that time.

"You have to trust your dance partner," Mr. Dig went on, addressing the entire class. "And what better way to build that trust than catching each other when you fall? So—pick a partner you trust."

Miranda tapped Lizzie on the knee. "Partner!" she said, smiling.

Lizzie smiled back and got to her feet. Then she put out her hand and hauled Miranda out of her sitting position, too.

Lizzie glanced over at Gordo for a moment, feeling slightly guilty. Who would he pick for a partner, now that she and Miranda were dancing together?

"Hey, Beth," Gordo said, walking over to a tall, quiet girl with dark hair, who was sitting at the edge of the bleachers. "Wanna be partners?"

Beth gave him a shy smile. "Okay," she said, giggling nervously.

Miranda and Lizzie stared at each other. "He picked Beth Ludberg?" Miranda asked.

Lizzie frowned as Beth stood up. Gordo barely came up to her chin. "Why would he pick her?" Lizzie wondered aloud.

"Okay, positions, everyone!" Mr. Dig called.

Lizzie took a place on the blue stretching mat a few feet in front of Miranda. "My life is in your hands," she joked.

"And . . . fall!" Mr. Dig called.

Lizzie let out a mock cry of fear as she fell into Miranda's arms. Miranda laughed as she caught her friend.

From the other end of the room, Lizzie heard a grunt. She looked over and saw Gordo at the end of the blue mats, struggling to hold up Beth Ludberg.

She and Miranda looked at each other and laughed. If Gordo was having this much trouble with a trust fall, they could hardly wait to see him dance!

Matt poked his head into the living room and saw that his mother was sitting on the couch, reading. He motioned to his best friend, Lanny, to follow him, and the two walked into the living room.

"Hey, it's *great* to see you again," Matt said smoothly as he took a seat on the couch next to his mother. "You're looking terrific."

Lanny plopped down on the easy chair by the couch and nodded encouragingly at Matt. Then he folded his hands in his lap and gazed at Mrs. McGuire. Lanny never actually *spoke*, but Matt and Lanny seemed to understand each other perfectly.

"Oh," Mrs. McGuire said, clearly surprised

at Matt and Lanny's sudden interest in her. Her hand flew to her blond hair, and she patted it self-consciously. "Thank you."

"So, tell us," Matt went on, his voice as silky as a TV announcer's, "what have you been up to?" He crossed his legs and gazed at his mother, as though he thought she were the most fascinating person on the planet.

Mrs. McGuire's forehead creased in confusion. "Well," she said, "I went to the nursery this morning and I bought some marigolds, then I planted them in the yard."

Matt lifted his eyebrows at this tidbit of information. "So, tell us," Matt said, "what was it like, working with the marigolds?"

Lanny leaned toward Mrs. McGuire eagerly. "Oh, you have to be really careful of the root ball," Mrs. McGuire explained. "Because otherwise they can die."

"So, you're saying it was *no bed of roses*,"

Matt said, winking at Lanny, who cracked up with silent laughter. Matt chuckled at his own joke for a minute, then turned back to his mother. "So," he said, suddenly serious, "is there any truth to the rumor that you and Sam McGuire are more than, shall we say, just"—he made air quotation marks with his fingers—*"friends?"* He lifted his eyebrows at his mom and leaned back in his chair, knowingly. "Now, be totally honest," he urged.

"Well," Mrs. McGuire said, slightly confused, "we've been married for fifteen years." She looked suspiciously at Lanny, then at Matt. "What's this about?"

"We're interviewing you," Matt explained, dropping his suave talk-show voice. "Lanny got a WebCam for his birthday, so we're starting our own talk show on the Internet. We premiere tonight."

Lanny grinned at Mrs. McGuire, and peered at her through the "camera lens" of his fingers.

"Wow—I think that's great!" Mrs. McGuire said, beaming. "And I would *love* to be a guest." She got up and headed toward the kitchen.

"Ooh," Matt said, holding up his hand, traffic-cop style. "I think we got our signals crossed. You see, we were only *practicing* on you."

Mrs. McGuire's face fell.

"You're not really what our target audience is looking for," Matt went on.

Lanny nodded and waved his hand dismissively.

Mrs. McGuire could only shake her head as Lanny and Matt strode out of the room. Her son and his friend had left her completely speechless.

CHAPTER TWO

"I decided not to get the leotard for dancing," Gordo said later that day. School had been over for an hour, and he, Lizzie, and Miranda were hanging together at the mall. "I'm thin and I have a big head—if I put on a pair of white tights, I'll look like a Tootsie Pop with hair."

Lizzie grinned. She had to admit that Gordo had a point—tights were definitely not his best look. "Ooh, let's go in here," she said suddenly. "You may not need a pair of tights, Gordo, but I do." She dragged Miranda and Gordo into a store called Heather's.

When they walked in, Lizzie spotted a bowl filled with candies sitting out on the counter. Next to the bowl was a sign. "Quit staring—you know you want some," Lizzie read aloud. "That sign knows me *way* too well." Lizzie picked a candy out of the bowl and unwrapped it.

Miranda hauled her handbag onto the counter and started shoveling candy inside.

After the third handful, Lizzie gaped at her friend. So did Gordo.

Miranda noticed their looks. "Hey, I want *some*," she explained. "Not *one*."

Gordo shrugged and looked around the store. "Maybe I should change my look," he said suddenly, noticing a rack of sunglasses.

He walked over and inspected a few pairs.

Miranda eyed him doubtfully. "I didn't know you *had* a look, Gordo."

"Maybe I should *get* a look," Gordo said. He turned back to the rack of sunglasses and picked out a pair of aviator shades. "How 'bout this?" he said, turning to face his friends. He squared his shoulders and drawled, "Excuse me, ma'am, I'm with the president's security detail. Please clear the area."

"Uhh, I don't think so, Gordo," Lizzie said, as she pulled open a cosmetics case. *Yeech.* Who wanted electric-blue eye shadow? She put the case back in the basket on the counter.

Gordo pulled another pair of sunglasses from the rack. "How about these?" he suggested. "Ciao, I am Aldo," he said in a phony Italian accent. "Come ride with me upon my Vespa. We will eat *gelati* in the moonlight."

Miranda rolled her eyes.

"Keep trying, Gordo," Lizzie said.

Gordo put back the Italian frames and picked out a pair with yellow rims. "Yo," he said in a deep voice. "My name is P. Diddy. How are you ladies doing this fine day?"

Lizzie giggled. She couldn't help it—Gordo was so white bread that he would have made a circle seem edgy.

"You know what?" Miranda said quickly. "I'm just going to go over there and check the lipsticks out." She ducked over to a rack on the counter as though she couldn't wait to get away from Gordo and his style identity crisis. Lizzie followed her and started looking through the silver tubes. Gordo stayed at the sunglasses rack, clearly absorbed by the endless choices.

"You know, flavored lipsticks are getting *so* out of hand," Miranda said, pulling a lipstick from the rack. "Now they have Mochaccino."

"I'll take a decaf, please," Lizzie joked.

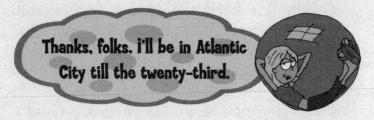

Thanks, folks. I'll be in Atlantic City till the twenty-third.

Lizzie spotted a display of cute sweaters in bright colors and wandered over to get a better look.

Miranda twisted open a lipstick and crinkled her nose at the color. Putting the cap on quickly, Miranda shoved the lipstick back into its slot. But she pushed too hard, and the rack wobbled a little. An avalanche of lipsticks tumbled to the floor. Miranda grimaced and grabbed the lipsticks, shoving them haphazardly back into the rack. "Um, Lizzie," she said over her shoulder as she walked away from the jumbled lipstick rack. "Let's just grab the tights and go, before Gordo over there turns into Tom Cruise." Miranda looked over at their friend, who was still engrossed in trying on every pair in the rack.

"Don't be in such a rush, Miranda," Lizzie said as she inspected a fuzzy maroon sweater. "We just got here."

Miranda shrugged and turned to go. But just as she was walking out of the store, a big, beefy hand landed on her shoulder. When Miranda looked up, she saw a heavyset security guard frowning at her.

"Excuse me, miss," the guard said. "Would you mind opening your bag, please?"

"What?" Miranda asked. "Why?"

Lizzie looked up and put her sweater back on the rack, frowning. Why was the security guard hassling her friend?

"Just open it, please," the guard snapped.

Miranda looked around. All the people in

the store had stopped what they were doing to stare at her. Miranda's face was burning as the guard reached for her bag. "No!" she cried, pulling it away.

"What is going on here?" Lizzie demanded as she joined Gordo at the sunglasses rack.

The security guard scowled at her. "It's about your friend here stealing lipstick."

"Okay, that's crazy, because I didn't steal anything," Miranda protested.

"I saw you knock over the lipstick rack," the guard said. "I don't think you put them all back." He grabbed her purse and started rummaging through it. His eyebrows raised when he saw the mass of wrapped candies inside, but he didn't say anything. He just shoved them aside and kept looking.

"Okay, I did not take any of your lipsticks," Miranda insisted. "I—"

Miranda's voice faded as the security guard

fished a shiny silver tube from her purse and held it up. "Okay, that's one of your lipsticks," Miranda admitted.

Lizzie gasped.

Miranda turned and faced her friend. "But I bought it here, like, last week," she explained.

"Then how come it looks new?" the guard asked.

"Maybe because I haven't used it yet," Miranda said. "I haven't finished my Decaf Mochaccino lipstick." She turned back to her friends. "Come on, Lizzie," she pleaded. "You were with me when I bought it."

Lizzie bit her lip. Yikes—what was she supposed to do? Miranda was her friend . . . but Lizzie didn't remember seeing her buy any lipstick the week before. "I don't think I was," Lizzie said weakly.

"You were outside, getting a pretzel, but we

were at the mall together!" Miranda cried.

Lizzie shook her head. She didn't know what to say. She loved Miranda, but Lizzie was a terrible liar. Lizzie knew that if she tried to cover for Miranda, they'd both get into trouble.

"Right," the guard said, grasping Miranda's shoulders. "I'm going to have to ask you to come with me." He steered her toward the back of the store.

"But she—" Lizzie started.

"Hey!" The guard cut her off. "I suggest you stay out of this, unless you want to come, too," he warned. "Let's go," the guard said to Miranda.

Lizzie sighed as the security guard led Miranda away.

"Sir!" Gordo called after the guard.

Miranda looked back at him, hopefully.

"I'm putting these back!" Gordo said, indicating the sunglasses in his hand. "I'm *not* taking them."

The guard ignored him, and Miranda just shook her head as he guided her into a back room. Lizzie couldn't believe this. First *The Red Pony*, then a crazy dance assignment . . . and now, her friend was getting arrested! Could this day possibly get any worse?

"Okay," Matt said as he showed his friend Jackson Myers around the set of his talk show. It wasn't exactly a Burbank studio. In fact, it was the McGuire garage, complete with racks of garden tools and auto parts in the background. Matt and Lanny had set up a couch and a chair in front of the WebCam, which sat next to a TV monitor and a computer monitor showing a map of the United States. "You look at the camera there, and the monitor shows how many people are watching,"

Matt explained to Jackson. "The more green dots, the more people. Okay, we start in a minute, so go outside over there, and come in and sit down, and we'll talk about your dad."

Jackson nodded, and his round face broke into a smile as he headed through the side door to the garage. Matt settled onto the sofa. Lanny sat down in a chair next to him, and Matt punched a button on the computer keyboard, then turned to face the WebCam. "Hey!" he said, smiling into the camera. "Welcome to *Matt After Dinner*. I'm here with my 'Councilman of Cool,' the one, the only . . . Lanny Onassis, everybody."

Lanny pointed both index fingers at the audience and winked.

"Okay," Matt went on, "our first guest is Jackson Myers, whose father is the one and only Mike Myers." Matt switched into a cheesy British accent, and added, "Very groovy, baby." He grinned. "I bet he's got a million interesting stories to tell us, so let's bring him out—Jackson Myers, everybody!"

Green lights began popping up across the map of the United States as Jackson shuffled through the door. Jackson smiled slightly and waved at the WebCam, until Matt steered him over to the couch.

"So, Jackson, tell us," Matt said, "is your dad going to star in another *Austin Powers* sequel?"

"Why would he?" Jackson asked. His eyebrows drew together in a confused frown.

Lanny cocked an eyebrow.

"Because he's Mike Myers," Matt prompted— "the actor who plays Austin Powers."

"Uh-uh," Jackson said, shaking his head. "He's Mike Myers, the dry cleaner. They have the same name."

Matt's jaw dropped open. "Dry cleaner?"

he repeated. He cast a quick glance at the map of the United States, and saw little green lights beginning to blink out. "Okay, it's been great having you!" Matt said quickly, practically yanking Jackson off the sofa. He shoved him out the door. "Bye!" He waved after Jackson for a moment, then turned to Lanny. "We've got twenty minutes to fill!" Matt whispered desperately. "We're losing audience. We need a guest!"

"Hey, guys," Mr. McGuire said from behind a shelf rack. He pulled a can off the shelf and started to walk away.

Matt turned to Lanny, smiling eagerly. Lanny closed his eyes, clearly disgusted, and shook his head.

"I know, Lanny, but he's better than nothing." Matt protested. Lanny sighed and shrugged.

"Hey, uh, Dad—" Matt called, "can you, please, be interviewed?"

"No problem," Mr. McGuire said. He walked over and sat on the couch, perching the can on his knee.

"So, I see you've brought something interesting to show us," Matt said, eyeing the black-sludge-encrusted can. "So what is that crazy stuff?" He grabbed his mug of water from the side table and took a quick sip.

"It's grease," Matt's dad said. "I'm going to grease the lawn mower, son."

Matt winced. "Are you going to run amok, charge all over the neighborhood, mowing everything down?" he asked hopefully. Matt glanced at the monitor, where a few more green lights had disappeared.

Lanny nodded eagerly, but Mr. McGuire just laughed. "No, no. I'm just going to trim the side yard—you know, it's getting kind of shaggy."

Matt's hopeful smile disappeared as more and more green dots winked out.

"And that's a difficult job," Mr. McGuire droned on. "So, you know, that's what I'm planning on doing." He wiped his nose, leaving a big black smudge on his face.

Matt giggled, and a few more green lights blinked on. Lanny laughed silently to himself.

"What?" Mr. McGuire asked, noticing their laughter. "Have I got something on my face?" He swiped at his nose again, leaving an even bigger streak on his face.

"Look at the monitor," Matt said, pointing to the TV.

"Have I got something on my face?" Mr. McGuire repeated as he peered at the image of himself that was being beamed live into homes across the country. Matt started laughing so hard that he spilled his mug of water in his father's lap.

"Son!" Matt's dad cried.

"I am so sorry, Dad!" Matt said. He stood

on the couch and reached toward the rack behind him. There was a clean rag on the top shelf.

"I mean, come on," Mr. McGuire complained. "I'm trying to do some lawn-mowing and stuff."

Matt pulled the rag from the shelf . . . but the rag was lying half under a large bag of potting soil. Matt gasped as the bag spilled open all over his dad.

Lanny was nearly falling out of his chair, convulsed with silent laughter. Matt was about to tell his friend that it wasn't funny, when his eyes landed on the map of the United States. Green dots were lighting up all over the place. "Dad!" Matt cried. "We're a hit!"

Mr. McGuire grabbed the rag from his son. "Give me that," he said, wiping the dirt from his glasses. But when the dirt was gone and he could finally see, he saw that the map of the United States was positively brilliant with spots of green light.

"Oh, my gosh," Mr. McGuire said with a gasp. "You're right!"

CHAPTER THREE

Lizzie was sitting cross-legged on her bed, trying to read, as Gordo kicked a Hacky Sack around. She sighed. It was no use . . . she just couldn't concentrate. How could she, when her friend was probably spending the night in a cold, damp jail cell somewhere? "What do you think they'll do to her?" Lizzie asked suddenly.

"I don't know," Gordo said, still kicking his Hacky Sack. "Shoplifting's a serious crime. I'd say . . . somewhere between a five-hundred-dollar fine, and busting up rocks on a steamy back road in Mississippi."

Lizzie grimaced. They wouldn't really send her friend to work on a chain gang . . . would they?

i like the exercise and being out in the sun, but baggy prison dungarees cut me across the hips.

Just then, the phone rang. Lizzie dove for the cordless on her bedside table. "Hello?" she said.

"I'm home." It was Miranda's voice.

Lizzie heaved a deep sigh. "That's such a relief," she said.

"What'd she say?" Gordo asked, catching his Hacky Sack. "Did they fine her? How much?"

"My parents finally came and got me," Miranda said. "*They* stood up for me."

Lizzie gulped. She knew that she probably could have done a better job of defending her friend, but she hadn't known what to do! After all, she hadn't been there when Miranda had bought the lipstick the week before. *If* she had bought it. "That's lucky," Lizzie said vaguely.

"Is it going to be all right?" Gordo asked. Lizzie held up her hand, gesturing for him to wait.

"It's not 'lucky.'" Miranda protested. "They *should* stand up for me."

"Well, yeah," Lizzie agreed—"of course. I mean, if you didn't do it."

"What do you mean, 'if' I didn't do it?" Miranda asked. "Of course, I didn't do it!" There was a pause. "I mean, you . . . you *do* believe me, right?" she asked.

"Um . . ." Lizzie said, fiddling with a loose string on her bedspread, "sure."

"You said, 'Um . . . sure,'" Miranda repeated. She sounded stunned. "You didn't say, 'Sure.' You said, 'Um . . . sure.'"

Lizzie swallowed hard, trying to think of something to say.

"You don't believe me," Miranda said, obviously hurt.

"Well. . . ." Lizzie hedged.

"Is it going to be all right?" Gordo wanted to know.

Lizzie ignored him. "Miranda," she began. "I mean, you *did* take all that candy, and you *were* at the lipstick rack, and then you wanted to leave so quickly, and it *was* in your purse . . ."

"And I told you why it was," Miranda snapped.

"Yeah, but Miranda," Lizzie protested, "the security guard said that he saw you. Who am I supposed to believe?"

"Well, you're supposed to believe *me*," Miranda said quietly. "And you don't." Miranda's voice was thick, as though she were about to cry. "Thanks for being such a lousy friend," she said.

Lizzie opened her mouth to say something, but the phone buzzed in her ear. A dial tone. Miranda had hung up. And Lizzie really didn't blame her.

Lizzie reached for the sky, then bent over to touch her toes. She was in gym class, warming up in her uniform—a pair of gray sweatpants and a blue T-shirt. Today, the class was supposed to practice the trust fall again; then the students were to spend the rest of the class period running through their dance routines with their partners.

Lizzie was feeling majorly nervous—her stomach was doing more flip-flops than the

Olympic gymnastics team. But it wasn't because she was about to have to practice her goofy dance routine in front of the entire class, which happened to include her crush boy, Ethan Craft. No, Lizzie was nervous because Miranda had been avoiding her all day. In fact, Miranda had positively dodged Lizzie at her locker, and had even pretended not to hear when Lizzie called after her. But now, they were going to have to dance together. Lizzie just wasn't sure how that was going to go. . . .

Gordo stood beside Lizzie, staring into space. How could he be so calm at a time like this? It was positively annoying.

"Gordo, shouldn't you be stretching?" Lizzie asked.

"Oh, uh . . ." Gordo laced his fingers together and cracked his knuckles. "There," he said.

"How can you be so casual about this?"

Lizzie demanded. "Gordo, you're getting ready to go up and do a routine. Aren't you afraid you'll flunk?"

"I'm sure it'll be fine," Gordo said calmly.

Lizzie sighed. "I wish I could say the same thing about Miranda," she said. "I mean, she hasn't even spoken to me."

Gordo lifted his eyebrows. "Well, Miranda can be a bit unreasonable at times."

Lizzie planted her hands on her hips. "How can you say that, Gordo?" she demanded. "I practically accused her of stealing!"

"Well, yeah," Gordo said, nodding. "You did kind of hang her out to dry."

"How can you say that, Gordo?" Lizzie shouted. "Just because I doubted her for one single second? I mean, the lipstick was in her purse!"

"You're right," Gordo said quickly. "The evidence *was* there."

"How can you say that, Gordo?" Lizzie was practically screeching now. "Miranda is my best friend, and I should know that she doesn't steal."

"Yeah, but . . ." Gordo gaped at her, obviously confused. "Whose side do you want me to be on here—yours or . . . yours?"

Lizzie exhaled in a whoosh. "I'm sorry," she said. "I know that I let Miranda down, and I didn't mean to. And now she's calling me a bad friend? You know, she's letting *me* down."

"Give it time," Gordo assured her. "It'll blow over. I'm sure everything's going to be cool."

Just then, Miranda stormed into the gym and walked over to Mr. Dig, who was in the middle of a windmill stretch. "Mr. Dig, I'd like another partner, please," Miranda announced, giving Lizzie an icy stare.

Lizzie's jaw dropped open, and she turned to Gordo. "You know, for a smart guy, you sure get a lot of stuff wrong," she told him.

Gordo rolled his eyes. "Eh, whaddaya going to do?"

"Okay, listen up," Mr. Dig announced. "Miss Sanchez feels that she can no longer work with her partner, so we're going to shuffle the deck a little." He scanned the line of kids doing warm-ups. "Cassie Pang," he announced, "you're with Miranda. Miss McGuire, you're with Ethan Craft."

Lizzie's eyes grew round, and her mouth dropped open. Could it possibly be true—was she really going to get to be Ethan's partner? Finally, her long streak of lousy luck was over—something good had happened!

Miranda wants to play it this way, fine. i'll fall into Ethan Craft's arms.

Mr. Dig clapped to get the class's attention. "Everyone, trust exercise!" he called, gesturing for the students to take their places.

Lizzie hurried to stand in front of Ethan. He gave her a smile, and Lizzie felt weak in the knees as she gazed into his blue eyes. This is like a dream come true, Lizzie thought as she sneaked a peek at Ethan's strong arms. She could hardly wait to fall into them.

This is working out all right.

"And . . ." Mr. Dig said, "fall!"

One by one, the kids in the front row fell backward. Cassie fell toward Miranda, who caught her with no problem. Beth caught Gordo easily. Lizzie took a deep, happy breath, and fell backward just as she heard

Ethan's voice behind her. "Whoa, there's a hawk with a mouse out there!"

Lizzie flailed wildly as she tried to keep herself from falling, but it was too late—she landed flat on her back. When she looked up, she saw Ethan staring out the gym window.

Maybe this isn't working out so well. Can't move. Oh, pain. Oh, the hurt.

Lizzie sat up and rubbed her shoulder. Cassie had just given Miranda a high five, and Miranda was grinning. But when she looked over at Lizzie, her smiled turned to a scowl and she folded her arms across her chest.

Ugh, Lizzie thought, as she stared at Miranda. It looked like her streak of lousy luck wasn't over, after all.

CHAPTER FOUR

"Hey, and welcome to *Matt After Dinner*," Matt said into the WebCam. He turned to Lanny, who was looking at him with raised eyebrows. "Now, I know what you're thinking, Lanny, 'cause you ask me every night— what did I have for dinner tonight? I had three sauerkraut chili-dogs and a root beer!" Matt let out a massive belch, and peered at the map of the United States on his computer, where little green lights were lighting up from New York to L.A.

Lanny frowned.

Matt angled his face away from the camera and leaned closer to his friend. "I know you think we're going for the cheap laughs, Lanny," he whispered, "but look at the green lights—this stuff sells!"

Lanny crossed his arms and stuck out his chin defiantly.

Just then, Mr. McGuire popped up from behind the couch. He was carrying two boxes. "Hey, guys," he said stiffly.

"Hey, look, it's a surprise guest!" Matt said as his father walked around to the front of the couch. "It's Dad. What you got there, Dad?"

"Well, son," Mr. McGuire said to the WebCam, "I have a box full of feathers, a few dozen whoopee cushions, and some old maple syrup." He grinned. "I'm working on a project."

"Well, let me give you a hand!" Matt said,

grabbing an open Tupperware container of maple syrup out of one of his father's boxes.

"Oh, no, don't take that. . . ." Mr. McGuire said. He tipped over the box, dumping a mass of whoopee cushions on the floor. "Give that back to me, son!" he protested, grabbing the maple syrup.

"Let me—" Matt protested, holding on to the maple syrup. "No!" he cried as he finally let go.

"Son, no!" Mr. McGuire shouted as he dumped maple syrup over his own head. Sticky syrup ran into his hair and down over his plaid shirt. "Oh, my gosh! Oh!"

"Look what you did," Matt said, shaking his head. He glanced over at Lanny. But Lanny wasn't laughing at the routine. He didn't even give them a tiny silent chuckle— he just stood there—stone-faced.

"Oh, gee whiz!" Mr. McGuire said, turning

the other box over his own head. White feathers cascaded down on him, and got stuck in the maple syrup. "Oh, my goodness. Uh, oh, oh boy, oh boy." Mr. McGuire stepped on a few whoopee cushions. They let out a series of very rude noises.

Lanny shook his head in disgust as green lights blinked on across the computer map of the United States.

Matt ignored him. "Aw, Dad," Matt said, stepping on a whoopee cushion, "you and your projects!"

"I know, son," Mr. McGuire said. "I just never learn!"

Lanny closed his eyes and stuck his nose in the air. Without a word, he turned on his heel, and headed for the side door of the garage.

"Lanny!" Matt cried. "You can't walk out!"

Lanny looked at him, then looked at Mr.

McGuire, who was still stomping gleefully on whoopee cushions. Lanny shook his head, clearly disgusted, and turned away.

"You and your precious dignity! You're just jealous you aren't the star!" Matt shouted as Lanny strode through the side door to the garage. "You'll be sorry! You're missing out on the big time!"

Mr. McGuire squeezed a whoopee cushion against Matt's head, and another green light lit up on the map.

Lizzie sat on the bleachers in the gym, her chin in her hands. Today was the big day—D Day. D, as in "dance." Lizzie was dressed in a pink sweater and jazz pants, but her partner was nowhere to be found. Not that she and Ethan had been able to practice their routine much. After Lizzie had fallen flat on her back the day before, her shoulder had hurt so badly that she had sat out the rest of the class. Now she wasn't sure what to do. Would she have to perform alone? She shuddered at the thought. It was too horrible to contemplate. Lizzie was almost positive that she would have a nervous breakdown if she had to attempt a solo fox-trot in front of her entire gym class. Lizzie never thought that she'd actually miss volley-ball, but she had to admit that it was sounding pretty good right now.

"Okay!" Mr. Dig called as he skipped—skipped!—into class with his boom box. How can he be so chipper? Lizzie wondered as Mr. Dig slid to a stop.

"Time to bust a move," he said to the class. "This time you *will* be graded. First up, David Gordon and Beth Ludberg."

"Good luck," Lizzie said to Gordo. She couldn't help smiling a little. Gordo and Beth had spent nearly all of their practice time sitting in a corner, chatting. Well, no matter what happens, Lizzie thought as she looked around for Ethan, at least my solo fox-trot will be better than whatever Gordo has planned.

Looking back on it, they might have been smart to practice at least, like, once.

Gordo walked to the center of the dance space, and Beth followed him shyly. Lizzie had to admit that Beth looked good. She was wearing a pink tank top, a gauzy black skirt, and pink pointe shoes. Hmm, Lizzie thought, eyeing the ballet shoes, interesting touch. The shoes made Beth look like a real dancer.

Gordo squared his shoulders as Mr. Dig pressed the PLAY button on his boom box, and classical music floated out. Beth raised her arms overhead and went up on pointe. Gordo struck a pose, and Beth twirled around him. As the music changed to a different tempo, Gordo changed his pose, bringing his hand to his chin and stroking it thoughtfully. Beth continued to leap and pirouette to the strains of the *Nutcracker Suite*.

Lizzie's mouth hung open. Gordo wasn't doing anything! He was just standing there while Beth performed a flawless ballet solo around him! Was anyone else seeing this? Lizzie looked over at Mr. Dig, who was smiling and leaning forward eagerly.

The music built to a big finish, and, at the final note, Gordo and Beth struck the same pose. Then Beth dropped into a graceful curtsy as Gordo bowed. "And we thank you," he said. He held out his elbow to Beth, who laced her arm through his. Together, they walked back to their seats in the bleachers.

The class burst into enthusiastic applause. Lizze had to admit that it had been a great performance. She clapped for them, too.

"Beth's mom has made her take ballet since she was eight," Gordo said, as he dropped into the seat next to Lizzie. "I knew she'd make me look good. She's got the footwork, and I've got the flair." He flipped his shaggy brown hair dramatically.

Lizzie giggled. Gordo may not be right all of the time, she thought, but when he's right, he is definitely right.

"Okay, next!" Mr. Dig said, placing a hand on Miranda's shoulder. She looked up at him and grimaced, and Mr. Dig smiled at her sympathetically. "Miranda's partner, Cassie Pang, has whooping cough," he announced. Then he looked over at Lizzie. "And Ethan Craft spotted a cloud he thought looked like a donkey, and ran face first into a beehive. He won't be joining us today."

Lizzie's eyes grew round. Wow, that was bad news about Ethan. And even worse— now she really *would* have to perform solo!

"So, I am forced to reinstate the team of Sanchez and McGuire," Mr. Dig went on.

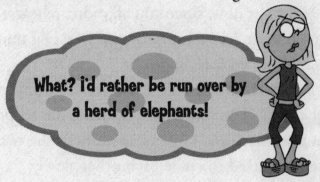

What? I'd rather be run over by a herd of elephants!

Lizzie gaped at Mr. Dig. She was about to protest, but her teacher was wearing his No Nonsense face. She sighed. It seemed like she didn't have any choice. She looked over at Miranda, who sneered at her. Fine, Lizzie thought, as she hauled herself out of the bleachers—if Miranda doesn't want to be nice, then neither do I.

Lizzie and Miranda walked to the dance floor, glaring at each other. When they reached the performance space, Miranda planted her hands on her hips, and Lizzie did the same. Neither of them spoke.

"All right now, since you all didn't rehearse, I'm going to let you improvise," Mr. Dig told them. "Let your feelings out."

Miranda scowled at Lizzie, and dropped her arms. "I'm surprised you trust me to be your partner," she said sarcastically, as the two friends started to circle each other slowly.

"Yeah?" Lizzie demanded. "Well, I'm surprised that you'd partner with a *lousy* friend."

"Oh, yeah?" Miranda shot back. "Well, a good friend would have stuck up for me."

Okay, that was the last straw! Lizzie had taken just about as much as she could from

Miranda. She grabbed her friend by the shoulders and gave her a good shake. "Oh, well, you're not little Miss Perfect, okay? You're always talking about how you sneak into the movies, and how you pretend to be sick from P.E.!"

"Oh, yeah?" Miranda asked. Her nostrils flared as she shrugged off Lizzie's grasp and grabbed Lizzie's arms. Lizzie let out a little squeak as Miranda swung her around in a viselike grip. "Well, I don't play sick just to get out of Larry Tudgeman's birthday!" Miranda cried. "Does that make *you* a thief?" With a triumphant smile, she stomped on Lizzie's toe.

"Ow!" Lizzie shouted. "No! And it doesn't make me a lousy friend, either!" She lunged at Miranda and bent her over backward, into a dip.

"Yeah?" Miranda screeched. "Well, I—"

"Ladies!" Mr. Dig interrupted. "I don't want to hear any talking, I want to see some *action*!" He gestured at them to get on with their dance.

Lizzie and Miranda glared at each other a moment, then Miranda shoved Lizzie away and straightened up. Lizzie lunged at her friend and grabbed her by the arm. Miranda tried to shrug her off again, but Lizzie clung tight. Miranda changed strategies and grabbed Lizzie's shoulders. Lizzie let out a cry and tried to twist away. Mr. Dig leaped in to separate them, but neither would let go.

"No, that's . . . too much interpretation!" Mr. Dig said. "C'mon, dancers—retreat to neutral corners. Retreat to neutral corners!"

Lizzie still wouldn't let go. There weren't any corners in the whole school that were neutral enough for her and Miranda!

* * *

Matt was sitting on the couch in front of the WebCam, wearing a pair of overalls and a straw cowboy hat, and shaking a bottle of carbonated water. His dad was sitting next to him, wearing a fake handlebar moustache and a broken flowerpot on his head. *Matt After Dinner* was live on the air, and Matt and his dad were in the middle of their looniest routine yet.

"This oughta help things grow back," Matt said, as the water fizzed and sprayed in his father's face.

"But vot about zeez gophers in my pants?" Mr. McGuire asked in a phony Dutch accent.

Lizzie wandered into the garage, carrying a basket of laundry, which she set on top of the dryer. She was expecting a call from Gordo, who was supposed to help her with her English homework, so she had the cordless phone in the basket, too.

"Oh, hey, a special guest—Lizzie, my daughter," Mr. McGuire said to the WebCam when he saw Lizzie. "Honey, why don't you come over here and say hi to the audience."

"Yeah, come on over, Lizzie," Matt urged, glancing at his bottle of seltzer. There was more than enough to give his sister a good squirt in the face.

Lizzie rolled her eyes. "I'd love to, except for, you know, I have to go sit in the kitchen and watch the chicken defrost," she said sarcastically.

"My sister, folks," Matt said to the WebCam. "I don't want to say she smells like feet, but—"

The phone rang, and Lizzie pulled it out of the basket and pressed TALK. "Hello?" She waited for a response. "Hello?" She frowned at the receiver. Weird. "No one's there," she said.

"That must be Lanny," Matt said, motioning for the phone. Lizzie tossed it to him. "Make it quick, Lanny—I'm on the air." He listened for a moment. "What?" Matt cried. "But you worked on that project for two whole days!" He shook his head. "Okay, I'll be right over—maybe we can fix it." Matt clicked off the phone and turned to his dad. "Okay, you can handle the closing monologue. I need to go help Lanny."

"What's up?" Mr. McGuire asked.

"A couple of his dad's peacocks ate his history diorama," Matt explained. "I gotta help him fix it."

The daisies in the flowerpot on his head bobbed as Mr. McGuire nodded sympathetically. "Okay." Matt handed him the bottle of seltzer and stood up to leave.

Lizzie gaped at her brother. "Matt, I thought you were mad at Lanny," she said.

Matt shrugged. "I am," he admitted. "But he's my friend. He needs me to have his back."

"Oh." Lizzie thought for a moment. "Well, didn't he walk right off your show?"

"So?" Matt asked. "My friend needs me. That's it, case closed, no questions asked." He dug his hands into his pockets and shuffled off the set.

"That's my boy," Mr. McGuire said to the WebCam, and took a swig of seltzer.

it's bad enough when my parents teach me about life, but when my skunk-head little brother is a better friend to Lanny than i've been to Miranda, then i've totally hit bottom.

CHAPTER FIVE

The next day, Miranda was in the hallway outside her English classroom. "Miranda!" Mrs. Stebel called. "May I speak with you a minute, please?"

Miranda turned to face her teacher. "Sure," Miranda said, hugging her binder against her chest. "What's up?"

"Well, let's step in here, please." Mrs. Stebel steered Miranda into the classroom. The teacher took a deep breath. "I read your report on *The Red Pony*, and it almost seemed like it was written by a professional," she explained, frowning slightly.

"Really?" Miranda said. "Hey, thanks!"

Mrs. Stebel shook her head. "No, you don't understand—I don't think that's good."

Lizzie walked by the classroom just in time to hear that last sentence. She peeked in and stopped short when she saw Miranda talking to Mrs. Stebel. Yikes! It sounded like they were having a pretty serious conversation. She hung back, uncertain whether to stay or leave. Was her friend in trouble? If so, Lizzie wanted to help!

"I'm hoping you didn't just buy the E-Z-Read condensed notes on *The Red Pony* and paraphrase their overview of the novel," Mrs. Stebel said to Miranda.

"Are you trying to say I copied my report?" Miranda asked.

Mrs. Stebel pressed her lips together grimly. "I'm saying you took a big shortcut," she replied.

Lizzie leaped into the classroom and blurted out, "No! She didn't!"

Miranda and Mrs. Stebel looked over at Lizzie, who plowed ahead. "Miranda is my best friend, and she doesn't lie, and she doesn't cheat, and I know that she doesn't steal." She bit her lip and looked at Miranda pleadingly. "And I was wrong to think that in the first place," she admitted. Miranda smiled, and Lizzie went on, "You know, I totally trust Miranda, and if she says she didn't do something, I'm going to believe her. That's it, case closed, no questions asked."

Miranda looked at her shoes, then back at Lizzie. "Thanks," she said quietly. She turned to Mrs. Stebel. "But I *did* use the E-Z-Read notes."

Lizzie's eyes widened in shock. "Oh!" she said, feeling a blush creep up her neck. "Well, then, you two just go along with whatever you were talking about."

And i'll just quietly bury myself.

"It's, just, I had a math test that day," Miranda explained to her teacher, "and a history paper, and a book report, and I just thought if I used the E-Z-Read notes, it would just tell me what the story was about."

"I want to know what *you* think about *The Red Pony*, not what the people at E-Z-Read think," Mrs. Stebel said.

Miranda looked at the floor and nodded. "So you want me to do it over?" she asked.

"By tomorrow," Mrs. Stebel said. "Good luck."

Mrs. Stebel gave Lizzie a knowing smile as she walked out of the classroom. Lizzie grimaced, embarrassed. But then Miranda looked up at her and grinned, and Lizzie felt a little better. "I'm sorry, Miranda," Lizzie said quietly as she walked over to her friend. "I should have believed you in the first place."

Miranda heaved a sigh. "That's okay," she said. "I mean, I know I do stuff that looks kind of bad sometimes, but you've got to know I would never lie to you."

"I know," Lizzie admitted. "And I should've known it at the mall, too. Miranda, you're always there for me. And from now on, I'm always going to be there for you."

Lizzie smiled, and Miranda smiled back. "Back at you," Miranda said. She jerked her head in the direction of the door. "Let's go."

Lizzie followed her friend toward the doorway, when Miranda stopped suddenly. The next minute, she fell over backward! Without thinking, Lizzie reached out and caught Miranda before she hit the floor.

"Good catch," Miranda said over her shoulder. "Way to have my back."

Lizzie giggled as her friend pulled her down the hall by the hand. She was glad to have her trust-fall partner back. After all, Miranda was someone that Lizzie knew she could always count on—no matter what. And that was what friendship was all about.

GET INSIDE HER HEAD

Lizzie McGUiRE